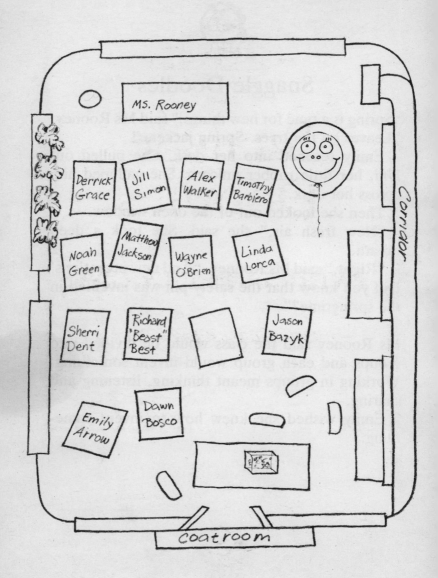

Snaggle Doodles

PATRICIA REILLY GIFF

Illustrated by Blanche Sims

Fontana Young Lions

327786
JS

First published in the USA 1985 by
Dell Publishing Co., Inc.
First published in Great Britain 1987 by
Fontana Young Lions
8 Grafton Street, London W1X 3LA

Fontana Young Lions is an imprint of
Fontana Paperbacks, part of
the Collins Publishing Group

Text copyright © 1985 by Patricia Reilly Giff
Illustrations copyright © 1985 by Blanche Sims

All rights reserved
Published by arrangement with Delacorte Press,
Dell Publishing Co., Inc., New York

Printed in Great Britain
by William Collins Sons & Co. Ltd, Glasgow

To Michelle Poploff

Chapter 1

"Who knows where the stationery room is?" Ms Rooney asked.

Emily Arrow dashed out of the cloakroom. "Me."

"Good," said Ms Rooney. "I need a box. Choose two helpers."

Emily looked around the room.

She loved choosing helpers.

Everyone was raising hands.

Everyone was saying, "Pick me, Emily. Pick me."

Everyone but her friend Richard Beast Best. And Matthew Jackson.

They were rolling pencils across their desks.

"I pick Jill," Emily said.

Jill Simon came up to the front of the room.

She had four plaits. Two in front. Two at the back.

She was fat and a bit wobbly. Like a strawberry jelly.

"And . . ." said Emily, "Linda Lorca."

Linda came up to the front.

She didn't have plaits like Jill.

She had a lot of thick brown hair.

She was always twirling it around her fingers.

"Now," said Ms Rooney. "Listen carefully. The box is in the corner. It's big and brown. It has INV written on it."

Ms Vincent, the student teacher, came to the front of the room.

"Do you want me to go to?" she asked Ms Rooney.

Emily looked at Ms Vincent.

She was beautiful.

Today she was wearing a pink skirt and a purple jumper.

Ms Rooney shook her head. "I think the girls can do it alone," she told Ms Vincent.

Emily raced out of the classroom.

Jill and Linda were right behind her.

They climbed the stairs to the third floor.

They banged open the stationery-room door.

It was pitch black inside.

Emily felt for the switch.

She flipped on the lights.

The stationery room was full. She could hardly walk.

"What a mess," Jill said.

Emily stepped over some boxes. She looked around.

A cardboard cannon stood in one corner. The top class had used it in a play last year.

In the middle of the floor were stacks of old reading books.

Baby reading books.

Emily picked one up.

COME AND GO, it said on the cover.

It was full of dust.

Suddenly the lights went out.

The door banged shut.

Emily blinked. It was too dark to see anything.

Behind her there was a sound.

A strange sound.

It sounded like a ghost. Or a monster.

Emily's heart began to pound.

Jill screamed.

The lights went on again.

"April Fool!" shouted Linda.

"Snaggle doodles," Emily said. She waited for her heart to stop pounding.

"I thought it was a vampire," Jill said. "A spooky—"

"I knew it all the time," Emily said. She crossed her fingers.

"It's April the first," Linda said. "Everyone tries to fool everyone else."

Emily didn't say anything.

She wanted to pull Linda Lorca's fat brown hair.

"That wasn't nice," Jill said.

"Don't be silly," Linda said. "Emily knew all the time."

Emily pulled an old flowerpot out of her way.

"Let's look for the box," said Linda.

"I'm looking," Emily said. "It's right here. In the corner."

Emily leaned over. On the top of the box was a big INV. "I told you," she said.

They pushed some other boxes aside.

Then they dragged the INV box across the floor.

"What's INV?" Jill asked.

Emily tried to think.

"Invitations, I bet," Linda Lorca said. "Wedding invitations."

11

"To Ms Vincent's wedding?" Jill asked. "It's a pretty big box."

"That's because Ms Vincent's going to ask a lot of people," said Linda. "Teachers. Not kids."

"Really?" Jill asked.

"Really," said Linda. "I know something else, too. Ms Vincent's new name. It's Mrs Stewart."

"How nice," said Jill.

Emily wanted to ask Linda how she knew so much.

But she kept her mouth closed.

She didn't want everyone to think she didn't know all about Ms Vincent's wedding.

Emily began to lift the box.

"Let me," Linda said.

"I think we should all take a corner," Jill said.

"I was the first one chosen," Emily said.

She lifted the box a little higher.

She could just get her arms underneath it.

She rested her chin on top.

She started walking down the corridor.

She took tiny little steps.

Jim the caretaker came along. "I'll carry that," he said.

"Good idea," Linda said.

"I can do it," Emily said.

"It's pretty big," he said.

"It's not heavy," Emily said.

"If you're sure . . ." he said. He turned the corner.

Emily stopped at the top of the stairs.

She had to catch her breath.

"I think we should help," Jill said.

"I think you're going to drop it," Linda said.

Emily shook her head.

The box slid out of her hands.

"Snaggle doodles!" Emily yelled.

The box banged down the stairs.

The top opened.

A load of things fell out.

Not wedding invitations at all.

Red and green paper. An old wheel. Pink balloons. A yellow plastic horn.

They dashed down the stairs.

"You should have let us help," Linda said.

"If we broke something . . ." Jill began. She looked as if she were going to cry.

Emily began to pick things up. A box of rubber bands. A bunch of old glass door knobs.

She tossed them into the box.

"Nothing's broken," Emily said.

She scrambled to pick up the box again.

She didn't want Linda or Jill to grab it first.

Ms Rooney would think it was great that she could carry it all by herself.

Next to her Linda sniffed. "Ms Rooney told all of us to do it."

"You've got dirt all over your face,"Emily said.

"Have I?" Linda asked.

She rubbed her nose.

"April Fool!" Emily yelled.

She opened the classroom door and marched inside.

Chapter 2

"Spring is a time for new things," said Ms Rooney. "Leaves on the trees. Spring jackets."

Emily reached into her desk. She pulled out Uni, her little rubber unicorn. She galloped him across her desk.

Then she looked out of the open window.

"New fresh air," she said. She took a deep breath.

"Right," said Ms Rooney. "And new inventions. Did you know that the safety pin was invented in the springtime?"

"And Coca-Cola," said Ms Vincent, the student teacher.

"And rubbers on pencils," Ms Rooney said.

"And cricket bats," said Beast.

"Really?" asked Ms Rooney.

Beast raised one shoulder in the air. "I made a guess," he said. "It's cricket time."

"We'll have to look that up," said Ms Rooney. "Good thinking anyway."

Emily put up her hand.

She was going to say that maybe bathing suits were invented in April. Or skipping ropes.

"We're going to make our own inventions," said Ms Rooney.

Emily put her hand down.

She didn't know one thing about making inventions.

Ms Rooney went to the blackboard. "We'll work together in groups."

Emily put up her hand again.

She knew about groups.

She had been captain of a maths group once.

Maybe Ms Rooney would let her be the head of an invention group.

"Not so fast, Emily," said Ms Rooney. She picked up a piece of chalk.

THINK, Ms Rooney wrote on top of the board.

LISTEN, she wrote next.

SHARE, she wrote on the third line.

She turned to the class. "That's how we work in groups," she said.

Emily wished Ms Rooney would hurry up.

She wanted to get to the inventing part.

"Yes," said Ms Rooney. "It's important to learn how to work together. Sometimes we can get more done and—"

Linda Lorca put up her hand. "If you have a big box to carry, and a couple of people to carry it" – Linda stopped to take a breath – "then it doesn't get dropped."

"Right," said Ms Rooney.

"Snaggle doodles," said Emily under her breath.

In front of Emily, Beast wasn't paying attention.

He pulled out a piece of paper.

Emily watched him draw a boy.

The boy was wearing cricket gear.

Then he drew a cricket ball.

The ball was landing on the boy's head.

"CLUNK," Beast wrote at the bottom of the picture.

Emily started to laugh.

Beast was laughing too.

"I hope you're listening," Ms Rooney told them.

Emily sat up straight.

She tried to stop giggling.

She wished she knew how to invent something.

"Now," said Ms Rooney. "I think we're ready."

She looked around the room. "Linda," she said. "You can be the head of the first group."

Emily looked at Linda.

Linda was smiling.

That Linda Lorca.

She loved to be the head of things.

Emily put her hand up quickly.

But Ms Rooney didn't choose her.

She chose Jason Bazyk and Wayne O'Brien for the other two groups.

"Snaggle doodles," Emily said under her breath.

She looked down at her desk.

She didn't want Ms Rooney to know that she had a cross face.

Next to her Dawn Bosco had a cross face too.

"I hope you remember what we said," Ms Rooney told them. "About groups, and working together, and leaders."

Emily nodded a little.

She didn't even know Ms Rooney had been talking about leaders.

Maybe that was because she had been watching Beast draw.

It didn't make any difference, though.

Ms Rooney hadn't chosen her to be a leader.

She had called on Linda Lorca.

Linda Lorca probably would be a terrible leader.

She hadn't even been captain of a maths group.

Chapter 3

Emily followed Linda to the back of the room.

She leaned against the science table.

Alex Walker and Matthew came back to the science table too.

"Is everybody here?" Linda asked.

"Of course we're all here," Emily said. "Four of us.

She wanted to say, "Can't you count?"

She didn't, though.

They might think she was angry because Linda was the leader.

Matthew leaned against the science table too.

Emily tried to inch away from him.

Next to Beast, Matthew was the nicest kid in the class.

But Matthew must have wet the bed last night.

Matthew wet the bed almost every night.

Linda Lorca was inching away from Matthew too.

Ms Rooney chose the rest of the groups.

Jason's group went to the front of the room.

Wayne's group sat on the side.

Ms Rooney opened the big INV box. "Let's see which group can make the best invention," she said.

Ms Vincent went to the front to help Ms Rooney.

A minute later she came back to Emily's group.

She dumped a pile of things onto the science table.

"This is my special month," Ms Vincent told them.

"Your wedding," Emily said.

"Yes," said Ms Vincent. 28th April."

"Are you having bridesmaids?" Linda Lorca asked.

"I've already asked that," Emily said. "A long time ago."

Ms Vincent smiled. "No bridesmaids." She went to the front of the room.

Emily thought about Ms Vincent's wedding.

She wished she were Ms Vincent's bridesmaid.

She'd be wearing a long pink dress.

She'd carry a basket of pink flowers.

She sighed.

She wished she could at least go to Ms Vincent's wedding.

"I hope I'm invited to Ms Vincent's wedding," said Linda.

Emily didn't say anything.

She looked at the things on the table.

A cardboard cereal box. Two pink balloons.

A red belt. A white plastic cup. Two black socks. A flashlight.

Matthew picked up a balloon.

He began to blow it up.

"Listen, Matthew," Linda said. "Let's not put our mouths on everything. There'll be germs all over the place."

Emily looked across the room.

Wayne's group was staring at a pile of stuff too.

Jill Simon had a pine cone in her hand. "I don't know what to do," she was saying.

She looked as if she were going to cry.

"Don't be a baby," Sherri Dent told her.

Emily looked back at her own group.

Matthew had put a green paper hat on his head.

He was playing a pretend drum.

Alex Walker held a dog's mask up to his face.

He began to make barking noises.

"Stop fooling around!" Linda yelled.

"Let's get started," Emily said.

"This is my group," said Linda. "I'm the one who says, "Let's get started.""

Linda was getting very bossy, Emily thought.

This was going to be a terrible group.

They'd probably have a terrible invention.

Emily pulled Uni the unicorn out of her pocket. She stood him next to the fish tank.

She wondered if Drake and Harry, the class fish, knew what a unicorn was.

At the front Ms Rooney clapped her hands.

"I hope you're off to a good start," she said.

"What a start," said Alex.

"No start," said Matthew.

Linda raised her hand. "I can't get everyone to—'

"This is a big project," said Ms Rooney.

"You'll have to think about it. Next week we'll work some more. And the week after."

Just then the bell rang.

Three times.

Three times more.

"Line up," said Ms Rooney. "It's a fire drill."

"Worse luck," Linda Lorca whispered. "I've just thought of a terrific invention. I've even thought of a name for it."

Emily lined up behind Linda.

She put her finger up to her mouth, "Shh."

Linda shouldn't be talking during a fire drill.

It was against the rules.

Emily marched out of the classroom.

She wished Linda were the head of someone else's group.

She wished she could think of a terrific invention.

She wished she could think of a name for it.

Chapter 4

It was Wednesday, the next week.

Playtime outside.

Emily marched under the climbing frame.

"Tum, tum, dc, tum," she said. "All dressed in white."

She pretended she was marching down the aisle.

The rest of the class were sitting on benches. They were smiling.

They thought Emily was the prettiest bridesmaid they had ever seen.

A little stick hit Emily on the head.

"Snaggle doodles," Emily said. She looked up.

Matthew Jackson was sitting on top of the climbing frame.

He was grinning at her.

Emily grinned back.

"What's this snaggle doodles stuff?" Matthew asked.

"I made it up," Emily said. "I like the sound of it."

"But what's it supposed to mean?"

Emily shrugged her shoulder. "I say it when I'm really cross . . . or worried . . . or really happy."

She stepped over Beast.

Beast was lying in the dirt. He was digging a hole to China with a stick. He had started it yesterday.

"Pretty good," Emily said.

"Up to my wrist," Beast said.

"Terrific."

"Not so terrific," Beast said. "I was almost up to my elbow last week. Jim the caretaker filled it in."

Emily leaned over. "Look at that great worm."

"I wonder if it's the one we saved last autumn," Beast said. "Remember? We took him out of a puddle."

"Maybe," Emily said. "He looks the same."

"All worms look the same," Matthew said. "Some are just a bit longer. Or fatter."

"Listen," Emily said. "I've been thinking of something all week."

Matthew threw another stick down.

"Are you listening?" Emily asked. "It's about—"

Just then Linda Lorca came over.

Jill was right behind her.

Today Jill was wearing thick white ribbons on her four plaits.

"Here comes the bride," Jill sang.

Emily sighed. "I'm trying to tell everyone my idea."

"Can I hear too?" Jill asked.

"Yes," Emily said.

Linda Lorca stuck her foot into Beast's hole. "Up to my ankle pretty soon," she said.

"If Jim doesn't come along," Beast said.

"My idea is this," Emily said. "Maybe we could bring a cake for Ms Vincent. A wedding cake."

"Good idea," said Jill. She picked up a stick.

She began to help Beast dig.

Linda Lorca frowned. "I had that idea first."

"Snaggle doodles," Emily said under her breath.

"I've even asked my mother."

"I'm asking my mother too," Emily said. "She bakes wonderful cakes."

"My mother told Ms Rooney," Linda Lorca said.

Emily picked up a stick too.

"Ms Rooney said my mother can bring the cake," Linda said.

35

Emily scratched at the dirt.

She wished she could hit Linda with the stick.
"I'm getting Ms Vincent a present," Emily said.

"Me too," said Linda. "A beautiful wedding present. My mother says it's the best."

"Snaggle doodles to your mother," Emily said.

"I'm telling Ms Rooney," Linda said.

Just then the bell rang.

Playtime was over.

Beast stood up.

He brushed his hands.

Matthew jumped off the climbing frame.

"I think I'm going to get Ms Vincent a wedding present too," said Jill.

"Me too," said Beast. "I hope I can find one for a pound."

"Is that all you've got?" Linda asked.

Beast shook his head. "No. I've nearly got two pounds. I'm trying to save for a computer."

Emily looked up.

Beast and Matthew ran to line up. Ms Rooney was clapping her hands.

"Don't tell Ms Rooney about Emily," Jill told Linda. "She didn't mean it."

Linda Lorca looked at Emily.

Emily pretended she was looking at Beast's hole to China.

"All right," said Linda after a moment.

They began to run towards the line.

Ms Rooney started for the steps.

They ran a little faster.

Emily was last.

She looked at Linda Lorca.

Linda's hair was bouncing up and down.

Her jacket was flapping.

Ms Vincent would probably love Linda's cake, Emily thought.

She'd say Linda's present was the best.

She might even ask Linda to be bridesmaid.

Emily could see Linda marching down the aisle.

She'd be twirling her hair around her finger.

Emily wished she could think of a wedding present. Better than Linda's.

Something wonderful.

Everyone would say it was the best.

Even Linda Lorca's mother.

Chapter 5

"Time for inventing groups," Ms Rooney said on Tuesday.

Emily had two more spelling words to do.

She had to write them three times each.

That would be six words, she thought.

She bent over her paper.

She wrote them down as fast as she could.

Then she read through her paper. She had spelt *please* without the last *e*.

She rubbed out three times. She stuck in three *e*'s.

At last she had finished.

She raced to her seat at the science table.

She was the last one there.

Linda Lorca was frowning.

"From now on," she said, "I hope people will be on time."

Emily didn't look at Linda.

She kept her eyes on the fish tank.

She watched Drake and Harry swimming around.

"Ms Rooney said to think first . . ." Linda began.

Emily picked up the cereal box.

It had a big red circle in the middle.

It said POW on top.

"Maybe we could make . . .' Emily began.

She stopped.

She couldn't think of one thing to invent.

"I forgot to think this week," Matthew said.

"I forgot too," said Alex.

"Well," said Linda, "you don't have to think. I've already thought."

Matthew slid down in his seat.

He was yawning.

Emily tapped the fish tank.

Harry swam over to her.

"We're going to make a tree," Linda said. "Just like a Christmas tree,"

"This is April," Matthew said. "Time for cricket."

"I know," Linda said. "We're going to call it an April tree. Cut up the box. Hang the balloons on it. The socks . . ." She looked around, smiling.

Emily kept looking at Harry and Drake. She was shaking her head at the same time.

"I think Jason's group is making a tree," Matthew said.

They looked towards the front of the room.

Jason's group had a brown stick. They were hanging paper towels all over it.

"How do you know that's a tree?" Linda asked.

Matthew raised his shoulders in the air. "It looks like a toilet paper tree," he said.

He and Alex poked each other. They started to laugh.

Alex picked up a sock. "Two holes in this," he said.

He poked his fingers through the holes. He wiggled them at Matthew.

"We could make a sock worm," Matthew said.

· They started to laugh again.

"I don't think an April tree is any good," Emily said.

"Stop fooling around," Linda told Matthew and Alex. She was frowning.

Alex wiggled his fingers at her.

· "Then we'll make a . . ." Linda began and stopped. "What's Wayne's group making?"

Emily looked towards the side of the room.

Dawn was covering something up.

A pile of yellow and purple plates stuck together.

"What's that?" Matthew asked.

"Who knows?" Linda said. "But everyone else has started something."

"We may never think of anything," Emily said.

"We're the worst," said Matthew.

"Right," Emily said. "The worst group in the class."

"That's because we have the worst people," Linda said. "Nobody listens."

"That's because we have the worst leader," Emily said.

She began to put the invention things in a row. She picked up an iron tool. "I don't even know what this is."

"You don't know what anything is," Linda said.

"It's a lock," said Matthew.

"No," said Alex. "I think it's food for a sock worm."

He grabbed the tool. He started to make growling noises.

Just then Ms Vincent walked past. "Having a little trouble getting started?" she asked.

"We can't think of anything," said Matthew.

"Inventing is hard," said Ms Vincent. She patted Linda's shoulder.

Then she went to the front of the room again.

Emily swallowed.

Too bad Ms Vincent didn't know that Linda was a rotten leader.

Too bad Ms Vincent didn't know the boys were fooling around.

Emily put up her hand. She wouldn't be a telltale. She'd just ask to go to another group.

Just then Sherri Dent's hand shot up.

Ms Rooney nodded at her.

"I want to get out of Wayne's group," Sherri said.

45

Ms Rooney frowned. "You're supposed to work together."

Quickly Emily put her hand down.

"Look how nicely Jason's group is working," Ms Rooney said.

Emily looked at Jason's group. They were throwing more paper on the brown stick.

"Snaggle doodles on Jason," she said under her breath.

Ms Rooney clapped her hands. "Time for art. We have to stop work for this week."

Emily went back to her seat.

She looked across at Linda Lorca.

Linda's mouth was wiggling a little.

Emily wondered if she was going to cry.

Maybe it was because no one liked her invention.

Her silly invention.

Or maybe it was because she wasn't a good leader.

Emily pulled out her art smock.

Suddenly she felt a little sorry for Linda.

It might not be as much fun being leader after all.

Chapter 6

Ms Rooney's class marched down the corridor to the art room.

Emily walked behind Dawn Bosco. "What's your group making?" she asked.

Dawn shook her head. "I can't tell. It's a secret."

Emily bit her lip.

"What's your group making?" Dawn asked.

"It's a secret too," Emily said.

They went into the art room.

Mrs Kara was waiting.

"We have a wonderful project today," she said. "We're going to make place mats."

"What's that?" Beast asked.

"You don't know what a place mat is?" Sherri Dent asked.

Beast shook his head.

"It's for under your plate," said Mrs Kara. "At dinner-time."

"Oh," Beast said.

Emily looked at him. She smiled.

She could tell Beast wasn't mad about place mats.

Mrs Kara had pieces of material in her hand.

Yellow squares. Pink squares. Ugly orange squares.

Emily tapped Dawn on the shoulder. "What colour—"

Mrs Kara frowned. "If you don't want to make a place mat, Emily—"

"I do," Emily said quickly.

She sat up straight

Mrs Kara began to walk around the room.

She gave a pink square to Wayne. Then a yellow square to Jason.

Emily hoped Mrs Kara wouldn't run out of pink before she had a chance to choose.

"Can I have two?" Dawn asked Mrs Kara. "One for my mother? One for my father?"

Emily frowned. She hoped Dawn wasn't picking pink.

Dawn picked one yellow and one pink.

Emily could see there was only one pink one left.

Emily tapped Beast on the shoulder. "What colour are you picking?" she asked.

Beast made a face. "Pink, I suppose."

"If you don't care . . ." Emily began.

"What colour, Richard?" Mrs Kara asked.

"I don't care," Beast said.

Mrs Kara gave Beast a yellow one.

Emily breathed a sigh of relief. "I'll have a pink one," she told Mrs Kara. "Please."

"Last pink," Mrs Kara said. "Everyone else will have to take yellow or orange.

A few minutes later Mrs Kara walked around again.

She gave everyone some coloured wool and a fat needle.

"Picture your place mat," she said. "Think of it on the table."

Emily closed her eyes. She thought of her pink place mat. It was on the kitchen table.

"Now," said Mrs Kara. "How will you make your place mat pretty?"

"I'm going to make a flower," said Linda.

"I'm going to write my name," Beast said.

Emily thought about writing her name too.

Then she had a wonderful idea.

She squeezed her eyes shut.

She could picture Ms Vincent's kitchen table.

Ms Vincent was having supper.

Ms Vincent was still wearing her wedding veil.

Snaggle doodles, Emily thought. This idea was going to be the best. She grinned.

Ms Vincent had a pink place mat under her plate.

Her name was written on it.

Emily frowned a little.

What was Ms Vincent's first name?

She poked Beast.

Beast turned round.

He was trying to get his wool into the needle.

"What's Ms Vincent's first name?" Emily asked.

Beast looked up at the ceiling. "Sally, I think."

"Sally?"

"Right."

"I used to know how to spell that," Emily said. "But now I can't remember."

"Spell what?" Matthew asked. "I'm a great speller."

"Sally," Emily said.

"Easy," said Matthew. "S-a-l . . ." He stopped

to think. "It has to have an *e* on the end.

Emily sucked on her blue wool.

She made it into a nice point.

Then she stuck the wool through the needle.

She squinted her eyes.

She stared at the pink square.

She'd put S-A-L-E across the middle.

Then maybe she'd put a flower on it too.

Emily stabbed her needle into the square.

It was going to be a wonderful wedding present.

Chapter 7

It was getting close to the wedding.

Ms Vincent was away today.

She was buying wedding shoes.

Emily was glad.

She could work on her S-A-L-E place mat.

She wouldn't have to hide it.

She took it out of her desk.

The *S* was finished.

So were the *A* and the *L*.

They looked a little wiggly.

One of the *A* legs was longer than the other.

But it was rather good.

She looked at it for another minute.

It was more than rather good.

It was excellent.

Snaggle doodles excellent.

She was ready to start on the *E*.

"Inventing time," Ms Rooney said.

Emily went back to the science table.

She took her place mat with her.

"Did anyone think of anything?" Linda asked.

"I forgot to think again," Matthew said.

"Me too," said Alex.

Emily made a long stick line for the *E*'s back. "I thought you were thinking," she said. "I thought we didn't have to think." She gave Linda a look.

Linda shook her head. "I'm not thinking by myself any more." She looked hard at Emily.

Matthew picked up the flashlight.

He turned it on and off.

"That's good," he told Linda. "You were getting too bossy."

"Bossy as a sock worm," Alex said.

He and Matthew began to laugh.

"I told Ms Vincent," Linda said.

Emily put down her place mat. "You mean you're a telltale?"

"What a leader we've got," Alex said.

Linda shook her head again. Her hair went flying around. "Not that way," she said. "I told her I didn't know how to be a leader. I told her we couldn't get started."

"Whew," said Matthew. "I'm glad you didn't say it was my fault."

Emily swallowed. "It was your fault a little bit. You and Alex keep fooling around."

Alex knelt up on his chair. "I'm not fooling around any more."

"Listen, Emily," said Matthew. "You didn't do anything either. All you keep saying is snaggle doodles."

"That's right," said Linda.

"That's right," said Alex.

Emily put her place mat down. She wanted

to yell snaggle doodles at all of them. She wanted to go back to her seat.

She sighed. "I suppose you're right," she said.

Linda twirled her hair around. "Ms Vincent said it's hard to work together," Linda said. "She said the leader shouldn't be bossy."

"That's true," Emily said.

Linda looked at her. "She said we have to work together."

"Linda's right," Alex said.

"That's what I'm thinking," Emily said.

For a moment nobody said anything.

They looked at the things on the table.

"A cereal box," Linda said.

"With POW on the front," said Emily. "What could we do with it?"

"Too bad there isn't any cereal in it," Matthew said.

"No messing about," Alex said.

"What else have we got?" Emily asked.

"The flashlight," said Matthew.

"This tool thing," Emily said.

"That's a spanner," said Matthew. "I asked my father."

He held it up.

"See," he said. He picked up a white plastic cup. "I can stick this cup in the spanner. Tighten the screw."

Emily looked.

The spanner was holding the cup tightly.

"Loosen the screw," said Matthew, "the cup drops out.

"Looks like a robot," Linda said.

"We've got robot socks," said Alex.

"And a red belt for him to wear," said Emily.

"And a cereal box for his stomach," Matthew said.

They looked at each other.

"Terrific," said Linda. "A robot. He'll have a

spanner for a hand. He'll be able to hold things . . ."

"Like a flashlight," said Matthew, "and a dog's mask."

"And a pink balloon head," said Emily. "Snaggle doodles wonderful."

"What's this for?" Alex held up the S-A-L-E place mat.

"That's not for the robot," Emily said. "That's for a present. It has Ms Vincent's name on it."

"Pam?" asked Linda.

"No. Can't you see?" Emily took the place mat. She held it up.

"That says S-A-L . . ." Linda frowned. "I can't . . ."

"*E* goes on the end," Emily said. "Sa-le."

Linda shook her head. "Two *l*'s and a *y* for Sally. Besides, Ms Vincent's name is Pam."

"But Beast said . . ." Emily began.

61

"Beast made a mistake," Linda said. "Sally is Mrs Miller's name."

Emily swallowed. Mrs Miller. The worst supply teacher in the school.

Alex and Matthew started to laugh.

"Emily's making a place mat for Miller the Killer," Matthew said.

Emily rolled the place mat up. She put it in the drawer of the science table.

She pretended she was laughing too.

She began to put the belt around the robot's stomach.

She didn't say another word.

She didn't want everyone to know she was about to cry.

Chapter 8

Everyone was running around the classroom.

Matthew had chocolate all over his face.

Beast was drinking Coca-Cola out of a paper cup.

Tomorrow, Tuesday, was Ms Vincent's wedding day.

Emily took a bite of cake.

Linda Lorca's mother had made it.

It was wonderful.

Ms Vincent would probably ask Linda to go to the wedding.

And Linda Lorca's mother too.

Emily sighed. She looked over at the reading table.

Presents were piled on top.

Ms Vincent had opened them right after lunch.

Linda really did have a great present.

It was a white vase.

It had a yellow rose on one side.

Emily had a present for Ms Vincent too.

Her mother had bought it.

It was a bowl for crisps.

It was green.

And ugly.

Just then Ms Rooney clapped her hands. "Time to show your inventions."

Emily went to the science table.

Linda pulled the cover off the robot.

He had a fat pink head.

Linda had drawn two blue eyes.

Alex had made a red Magic Marker smile.

The robot's spanner arm was holding a white paper cup.

"This is the Snaggle Doodles Robot," Linda said. "He can hold things by himself."

"That's a terrific name," said Ms Vincent.

"It was Emily's idea," Linda said.

"What does it mean?" Ms Rooney asked.

"Being happy," Emily said. "Or cross . . . or anything you want it to."

"Wonderful," said Ms Vincent.

Everybody clapped.

Then Jason's group showed their invention. It was a tree.

A paper tree.

Wayne's group had a tree too.

It was a plate tree.

"Excellent work," Ms Rooney said. "Everyone tried hard."

Ms Rooney looked at Ms Vincent. "Time for the surprise, I think."

Ms Vincent went to the front of the room.

Her face was pink. She was smiling.

"I spoke to Mr Mason, the headmaster," she said. "And then I spoke to Ms Rooney."

Suddenly Emily knew what Ms Vincent was going to say.

She crossed her fingers.

She crossed her toes.

"Everyone is invited to the church," said Ms Vincent. "Please come to my wedding."

Ms Rooney was nodding her head. "I'll bring the whole class."

"Wow," said Beast. "No maths tomorrow. No spelling."

"I'll have to get a new dress this afternoon," Dawn said.

Emily smiled. She'd wear her best dress. And her shiny black shoes. She hoped she could find them in her cupboard.

Tomorrow would be a perfect day.

She was finally going to a wedding.

Their invention was the best.

If only she had had a good present for Ms Vincent.

She took another piece of cake.

Linda and Alex and Matthew were standing around the robot.

She went over to them.

"Hey," Linda said suddenly.

She looked at Emily. "I've just thought of something."

Linda's always thinking of things," Matthew said.

Linda looked around. "It's a secret, though."

Emily moved a little closer.

Linda pulled something out of the science table drawer. "Wait till you hear this idea, Emily," she said. "It's the greatest."

Chapter 9

Emily looked around the room.

Everyone looked different today.

"That's a nice blue suit," Emily told Beast.

Beast shrugged his shoulder. "My mother made me wear it. I wanted to wear black trousers."

"We're going to leave in two minutes," Ms Rooney said. "I hope everyone is ready."

"I'm ready," Matthew said. He was wearing his same old T-shirt. But today he had on a tie. It was green with little red dots.

"I'll be ready in one minute," Beast said.

He bent over his desk. He was drawing a picture of a bride and groom.

The bride looked like Ms Vincent.

Dawn leaned over. "How do you like my dress? It's brand new."

"It's the best in the class," Sherri Dent said.

Emily nodded a little.

She didn't care.

She was wearing her pink party dress.

There was a little ice-cream stain on the skirt.

But her mother said you could hardly see it.

The main thing was they were going to the wedding.

Ms Vincent's wedding.

Emily pulled the parcel out of her desk.

It was wrapped in white paper.

It had a pink ribbon on top.

Emily was going to give it to Ms Vincent after the wedding.

Emily smiled at Linda Lorca.

She waved the parcel around a little.

She and Linda had worked for an hour after school.

They had worked on the S-A-L-E place mat.

It didn't say S-A-L-E any more.

It said S-N-A-G-G-L-E.

Underneath, instead of a flower, was a big D.

D for doodles.

Ms Rooney told them to line up.

Emily walked around the science table.

She smiled at the robot.

He looked as if he were smiling back.

Ms Rooney's class marched down the corridor.

Mr Mason, the headmaster, waved at them.

"Say good luck to Ms Vincent," he called.

They went out of the door and down the street.

The sun was shining.

Emily took Uni out of her pocket.

Even Uni was going to see this wedding.

They crossed Linden Avenue.

They went into the churchyard.

Ms Rooney put her finger on her lips. "Don't make too much noise," she said.

They marched into the church.

Emily blinked a little at the darkness.

She let Beast and Matthew go ahead of her.

She had a seat right on the end.

Linda Lorca had a seat on the end too.

She was one row in front of Emily.

She turned round. "I like the music, don't you?"

Emily nodded. "I wanted to tell you," she said. "You were a great leader."

"Thanks," Linda said. "You were great too."

Just then the music stopped for a minute.

Then it started up again.

"Here comes the bride," the organ played.

Emily turned round.

Ms Vincent was coming down the aisle.

Her dress was white. It had a row of lace on the bottom.

She was wearing a tiny white hat.

It had a puffy veil.

She was carrying white flowers.

Emily had never seen anyone more beautiful.

She couldn't wait until she was a bride too.

Emily leaned out into the aisle a little.

She wanted to make sure Ms Vincent would see her pink party dress.

Ms Vincent did. She smiled.

She stopped for a minute.

She looked at Emily.

"Snaggle doodles," she said.

Patricia Reilly Giff

The Beast in Ms Rooney's Room
Fish Face
The Pop Corn Contest
December Secrets
In the Dinosaur's Paw
The Valentine Star

Illustrated by Blanche Sims

Meet the kids of the Polk Street School, and in particular the kids in Ms Rooney's class.

Among them are Richard 'Beast' Best, who has been kept back a year and is feeling a bit miserable; Emily Arrow, who is a poor reader but a fast runner; Dawn Tiffanie Bosco, the new girl, whom Emily isn't quite sure about to begin with; and chubby Jill Simon, the crybaby. Well, that's what Emily says.

Something is happening every month in their class, like having a pop corn contest, a ride in the fire engine, measuring up dinosaurs, or making presents for special friends.

Read all about what Ms Rooney's class gets up to. And there are more stories to come!

Simon and the Witch

MARGARET STUART BARRY

Simon's friend the witch lives in a neat, semi-detached house with a television and a telephone, but she has never heard of Christmas or been to the seaside. However, she has a wand, which she loses, causing confusion at the local constabulary, and a mean-looking cat called George, who eats the furniture when she forgets to feed him. The witch shows Simon how to turn the school gardener into a frog, and she and her relations liven up a hallowe'en party to the delight of the children and the alarm of the local dignitaries. With a witch for a friend, Simon discovers, life is never dull.

Very highly recommended by ILEA's *Contact* magazine: '. . . who could resist such a lively character?'

You will find more adventures of Simon and the Witch in *The Return of the Witch*, *The Witch of Monopoly Manor* and *The Witch on Holiday*, all in Fontana Lions.

Sunshine Island
Moonshine Baby

Clare Cherrington

illustrated by Jennifer Northway

Sarah is determined to be a cowboy when she grows up.
She hates sewing. But when she has to stay at home
after having her tonsils out, the sewing ladies tell her
stories about some faraway islands. The way they talked
you would think there was a different sun and moon
there. Soon, there was nothing that would keep Sarah
away from the sewing circle and from hearing about
girls who grew up in the West Indies long ago.

The Paddington Books

MICHAEL BOND

Paddington is a *very* rare bear indeed! He'd travelled all the way from darkest Peru (with only a jar of marmalade, a suitcase and his hat) when the Brown family first met him on Paddington Station. Since then their lives have never been quite the same . . . for things just seem to *happen* to Paddington – chaotic things.

What *other* bear could turn his friend's wedding into an uproar by getting the wedding ring stuck on his paw? Or glue himself to his dancing partner's back with his marmalade sandwich? *Only* Paddington . . . but as he says himself, 'Oh dear, I'm in trouble again.'

'Within a comparatively short time, Paddington has joined Pooh as one of the great bears of children's literature.' *The Teacher*

Paddington's own particular brand of chaos comes up often in Fontana Lions – in *A Bear Called Paddington, More About Paddington, Paddington Goes to Town, Paddington Helps Out, Paddington at Large, Paddington Abroad, Paddington Takes the Air, Paddington Marches On, Paddington at Work, Paddington on Top, Paddington Takes the Test, Paddington's Blue Peter Story Book* and *Paddington on the Screen.*

The Boy Who Sprouted Antlers

JOHN YEOMAN AND QUENTIN BLAKE

'As long as you set your mind on it and try hard enough, there's nothing you can't do,' said Miss Beddows to Billy when he declared that he simply couldn't make a basket. Billy liked the idea that he could do anything, but Melanie and Paul didn't agree.

'What about growing horns?' said Melanie. It was a challenge that Billy had to accept.

'Wildly improbable and cleverly sustained.'   *Margery Fisher*

Hilarious reading for sevens and up.

Cat Walk

Mary Stolz

illustrated by Erik Blegvad

Right from the start the little black barn kitten with the enormous white paws was different from the others. He also had aspirations. He wanted a name. He gets one from young Missy, the farmer's daughter, and a home. But when she dresses him up in dolls clothes and takes him for rides in the pram, it's time to move on – to another home.

This is an old story, disarmingly told, of a cat's progress from pillar to post, and beautifully illustrated.